Awesome Animals of ANTARCTICA

The Continent and Its Creatures Great and Small

Tamra B. Orr

Curious Fox Books

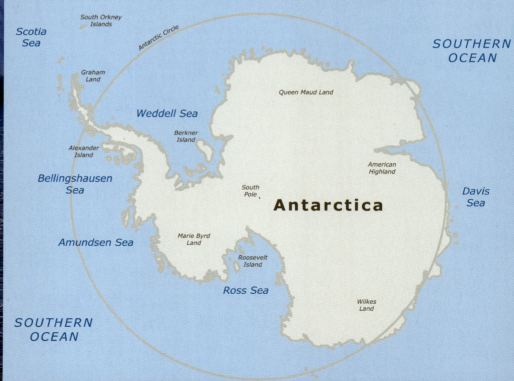

Welcome to Antarctica (ant-AR-tih-kah)! Brrrrr. Zip up your coat! This is the coldest biome in the world. Temperatures have gone as low as −128.6°F (−89.2°C).

Antarctica surrounds the South Pole. It may look large on a map, but Antarctica is smaller than South America.

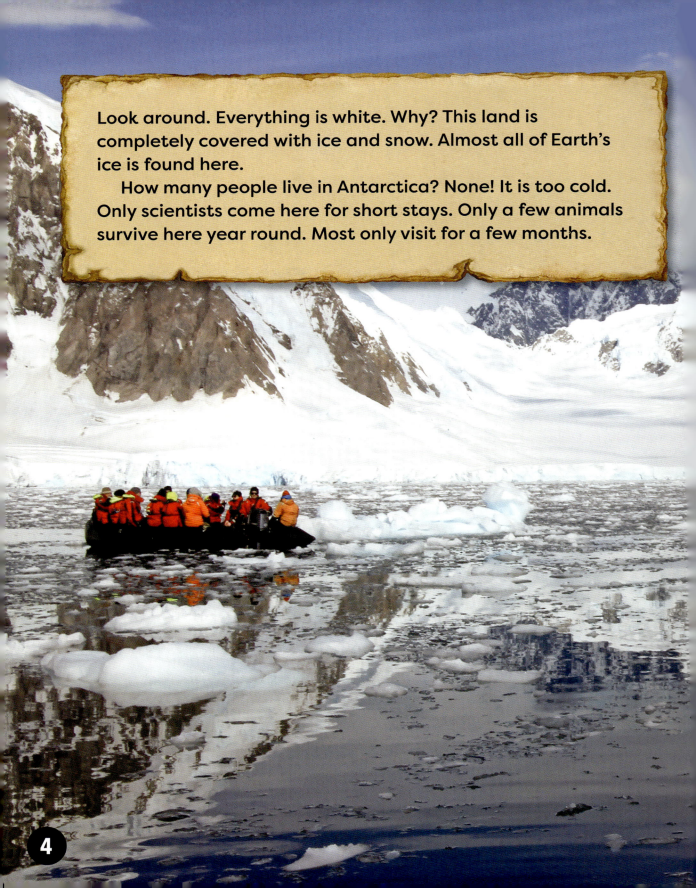

Look around. Everything is white. Why? This land is completely covered with ice and snow. Almost all of Earth's ice is found here.

How many people live in Antarctica? None! It is too cold. Only scientists come here for short stays. Only a few animals survive here year round. Most only visit for a few months.

In summer, green moss appears. It is too cold for trees and other plants to grow.

Some birds come to Antarctica to make nests and lay eggs. The gray bird with black-tipped feathers is a fulmar. Don't go too close to it! These birds can spit a terrible-smelling oil up to 5 feet (1.5 meters). They can also smell fish oil on the ocean surface, helping them to hunt fish.

SOUTHERN FULMAR
Wingspan: 4 feet (1.2 meters)
Weight: 28 ounces (794 grams)
Habitat: coasts by cool waters of the Southern Hemisphere
Diet: krill, crabs, squids, and fish

SNOWY ALBATROSS
Wingspan: 11 feet (3.4 meters)
Weight: 26 pounds (11.8 kilograms)
Habitat: coasts by cool waters of the Southern Hemisphere
Diet: crabs, squids, and fish

The albatross (AL-beh-tross) can fly more than 500 miles (800 kilometers) in just one day. It would take a car on the highway, taking no breaks, about 8 hours to go that far. It uses the wind currents and almost never flaps its wings.

ARCTIC TERN
Wingspan: 33 inches (84 centimeters)
Weight: 4½ ounces (128 grams)
Habitat: coasts of Antarctica and the Arctic tundra
Diet: fish and crabs

Arctic terns are big travelers. They will fly from the Arctic (North Pole) to Antarctica (South Pole) all in one year. The average Arctic tern will travel 44,000 miles (70,800 kilometers) every year. No other animal has as a longer migration than them!

The south polar skua (SKEW-ah) is known for its aggressive behavior. They have pecked and dived at scientists researching Antarctic animals. Skuas can even recognize people based on clothing they wear. But these attacks are just to protect their nests.

SOUTH POLAR SKUA

Wingspan: 4½ feet (1.4 meters)
Weight: 3 pounds (1.4 kilograms)
Habitat: coasts of Antarctica and Antarctic islands
Diet: eggs, fish, and krill

EMPEROR PENGUIN
Height: 4 feet (1.2 meters)
Weight: 100 pounds (45 kilograms)
Habitat: coasts and icebergs of Antarctica
Diet: fish, squids, and krill

What is that, waddling across the ice? It's a penguin! There are six types in Antarctica. The largest is the emperor (EM-per-er). Penguins swim fast, using their wings like flippers to dive deeply in search of food. They have waterproof feathers and webbed feet.

When the females lay eggs, the emperor penguins do not build nests. Instead, they cuddle. Their bodies have extra layers of fat that keep the eggs warm. The male emperor penguin takes care of his baby when the mother is away.

MACARONI PENGUIN
Height: 28 inches (70 centimeters)
Weight: 11 pounds (5 kilograms)
Habitat: coasts of Antarctic islands
Diet: fish, squids, and crabs

One of the most striking penguins is the macaroni penguin. Its name comes from the yellow feathers on its head and the rhyme "Yankee Doodle" ("stuck a feather in his cap and called it macaroni"). Male macaroni penguins will sometimes fight by knocking their large beaks against one another.

Adélie (AH-dell-ee) penguins migrate with the ice in the winter. As Antarctica freezes and expands every year, these penguins stay by the water edge. This way, they can swim in the water and hunt for krill.

ADÉLIE PENGUIN
Height: 29 inches (74 centimeters)
Weight: 18 pounds (8.2 kilograms)
Habitat: coasts and icebergs of Antarctica
Diet: fish, squids, and krill

Six types of seals live in the Southern Ocean around Antarctica. The most common is the crabeater. They actually don't eat crabs but live on krill. Crabeater seals spend time with their families on large blocks of ice.

Krill grow up to 2 inches (5 centimeters) in Antarctica.

CRABEATER SEAL
Length: 8 feet (2.5 meters)
Weight: 500 pounds (227 kilograms)
Habitat: icebergs of Antarctica
Diet: krill

A leopard seal stands out from other seals thanks to its spots. But watch out! It has very sharp teeth and a strong jaw.

Male leopard seals will "sing" underwater to attract females by making different sounds. They might even sing for hours!

The fur seal is smaller than the other seals in Antarctica. While other seals rely on fat to keep out the cold, these seals have thick fur to stay warm. A fur seal is quite the swimmer. It can dive as deep as 820 feet (250 meters), which is about 82 flights of stairs. It can also stay underwater up to five minutes before needing air.

ANTARCTIC FUR SEAL
Height: 6½ feet (2 meters)
Weight: 463 pounds (210 kilograms)
Habitat: coasts of Antarctic islands
Diet: krill, fish, squids, and penguins

The biggest animals in Antarctica are hidden beneath the waves. Many types of whales swim to the Southern Ocean. One is the sperm whale, which has the largest brain in the world. Baby sperm whales are 13 feet (4 meters) long and weigh 2,200 pounds (1,000 kilograms).

Sperm whales have teeth. They sometimes eat giant squid by diving down to 7,400 feet (2,250 meters) under the water.

SPERM WHALE

Length: 52 feet (16 meters)
Weight: 90,000 pounds (40,823 kilograms)
Habitat: cool waters of the world's oceans
Diet: squids, octopuses, and fish

ORCA

Length: 33 feet (10 meters)
Weight: 22,000 pounds (9,979 kilograms)
Habitat: oceans of the world
Diet: seals, sea lions, fish, squids, and whales

The orca is known as a killer whale, but it's actually a large dolphin. Orcas live in groups called pods. When in a group, they can hunt any animal in the water. This is why they have the nickname "the wolves of the ocean." A pod is made up of a family of orcas, up to four generations! Mother and baby orca whales often stay together for their whole lives.

BLUE WHALE

Length: 110 feet (33.5 meters)
Weight: 330,000 pounds (149,685 kilograms)
Habitat: oceans of the world
Diet: krill

The biggest animal on Earth spends time in Antarctic waters. The blue whale is long, about the length of a basketball court. When it comes to the surface of the ocean and exhales, the spray from its blowhole soars as high as 40 feet (12 meters)! That's almost 4 stories in a building.

There are other animals who have adapted uniquely to the cold. The only insect native to the continent is the Antarctic midge. It spends most of its life frozen in ice, living for about a week.

The Antarctic icefish has special blood to help it live in very cold temperatures. It doesn't have scales.

There are "spiders" in Antarctica, but you won't find them on the ice. They live in the sea looking for food. Sea spiders grow larger in Antarctica and in the deep ocean. They can be as big as a dinner plate.

ANTARCTIC MIDGE
Length: ¼ inch (6 millimeters)
Habitat: coasts of Antarctic Peninsula
Diet: algae and moss

ANTARCTIC ICEFISH
Length: 28 inches (71 centimeters)
Weight: 8 pounds (3.6 kilograms)
Habitat: cold waters of Southern Ocean
Diet: fish, crabs, and krill

SEA SPIDER
Length: 1 foot (31 centimeters)
Weight: ⅓ ounce (10 grams)
Habitat: near coasts of Southern Ocean
Diet: worms, jellyfish, and sponges

Penguins often look like they are playing as they slide across the ice and snow.

The ice and snow of Antarctica are not comfortable for people. But for certain animals, it truly is home sweet frozen home.

These leopard seals are clearly happy in this cold world!

FURTHER READING

Books

Cowcher, Helen. *Antarctica*. New York: Square Fish, 2009.

Jenkins, Martin. *The Emperor's Egg*. Paradise, CA: Paw Prints Press, 2009.

Kurkov, Lisa. *ICY! Antarctica*. Nigeria: Spectrum, 2014.

Saxon, Liam. *A Smart Kids Guide to Abundant Antarctica*. Thought Junction Publishing, 2015.

Viva, Frank. *A Trip to the Bottom of the World with Mouse*. Jackson, TN: Toon Books, 2012.

Websites

Globe Trottin' Kids: Antarctica
   https://www.globetrottinkids.com/antarctica

Antarctic Webcams and Timelapse Video
   http://www.antarctica.gov.au/webcams

Active Wild: Antarctica Facts for Kids
   https://www.activewild.com/antarctica-facts-for-kids

GLOSSARY

algae (AL-jee)—Simple plants that do not have roots, stems, leaves, or flowers. They generally live in water, in large groups.

arctic (ARK-tik)—Very cold areas near Earth's north and south poles.

biome (BY-ohm)—Any major region that has a specific climate and supports specific animals and plants.

blowhole (BLOH-hole)—A hole on top of a whale's head used for breathing.

continent (KON-tih-nunt)—One of the seven great pieces of land on Earth.

current (KER-ent)—A constant movement of water or wind in the same direction.

exhale (EX-hayl)—To breathe out.

krill (KRIL)—Very small creatures in the ocean.

migration (my-GRAY-shun)—When an animal moves from one place to another, usually for better weather.

pod (POD)—A group of ocean animals.

PHOTO CREDITS

Inside front cover (map)—Shutterstock/DidGason; inside front cover (animals)—Shutterstock/ruboart; p. 1—Christopher Michel; p. 2 (Antarctica map)—Shutterstock/Martyna Nawrocka; p. 2 (world map)—Shutterstock/Maxger; pp. 2-3—Andreas Kambanis; pp. 4-5—Shutterstock/reisegraf.ch; p. 5 (penguin)—Shutterstock/Tarpan; p. 6 (southern fulmar)—Shutterstock/juan68; pp. 6-7—Shutterstock/robert mcgillivray; pp. 8-9—Shutterstock/Dave Head; p. 9 (skua)—Shutterstock/juan68; pp. 10-11—Shutterstock/vladsilver; p. 11 (inset)—Shutterstock/Jan Martin Will; p. 12 (inset)—Shutterstock/RobJ808; pp. 12-13—Shutterstock/Anton_Ivanov; pp. 14-15 (all photos)—Liam Quinn; p. 15 (krill)—Shutterstock/lego 19861111; p. 16 (inset)—Shutterstock/Tarpan; pp. 16-17—Shutterstock/ViktoriaIvanets; p. 18 (inset)—Shutterstock/Anton Rodionov; pp. 18-19—Shutterstock/Stas Zakharov Photo; pp. 20-21—Shutterstock/ohrim; pp. 22-23—Shutterstock/Daniel Toh; p. 23 (inset)—Shutterstock/Anass Khrifi; pp. 24-25—Shutterstock/Sujan Maahmud; p. 25 (inset)—Shutterstock/Wirestock Creators; p. 26 (icefish)—Nature Picture Library /Alamy Stock Photo; pp. 26-27—Shutterstock/Simon Brockington; pp. 28-29—Shutterstock/nwdph; p. 29 (seals)—Shutterstock/Goinyk Production; inside back cover—Shutterstock/ruboart; back cover—Shutterstock/ruboart.

All other photos—Public Domain. Every measure has been taken to find all copyright holders of material used in this book. In the event any mistakes or omissions have happened within, attempts to correct them will be made in future editions of the book.

CHECK OUT THE OTHER BOOKS IN THE AWESOME ANIMALS SERIES

Awesome Animals of Africa
Awesome Animals of Asia
Awesome Animals of Australia
Awesome Animals of Europe and the United Kingdom
Awesome Animals of North America
Awesome Animals of South America

© 2024 by Curious Fox Books™, an imprint of Fox Chapel Publishing Company, Inc., 903 Square Street, Mount Joy, PA 17552.

Awesome Animals of Antarctica is a revision of *The Animals of Antarctica*, published in 2017 by Purple Toad Publishing, Inc. Reproduction of its contents is strictly prohibited without written permission from the rights holder.

Paperback ISBN 979-8-89094-105-3
Hardcover ISBN 979-8-89094-106-0

Library of Congress Control Number: 2024933038

To learn more about the other great books from Fox Chapel Publishing, or to find a retailer near you, call toll-free 800-457-9112 or visit us at *www.FoxChapelPublishing.com*.

We are always looking for talented authors. To submit an idea, please send a brief inquiry to acquisitions@foxchapelpublishing.com.

Fox Chapel Publishing makes every effort to use environmentally friendly paper for printing.

Printed in China